This book belongs to

"I love P.E.!" shouts Henry.
It's my favorite!"
In art class, he draws about dancing.

GOOAL!

In music, he sings about soccer.

And during math, he calculates the number of curl ups he can do.

But when P.E. rolls around, Henry has one

BIG PROBLEM...

...Manny the Monster.

"SURPRISE!"

"Not again!" yells Henry.

"We don't shout at our classmates," says Mr. Evans. "That's STRIKE ONE!"

"But it's Manny. He's the monster who always tells me the opposite."

"No excuses," says Mr. Evans. "Three strikes and you're in the safe zone."

"Eyes and ears on me," says Mr. Evans. "In the four corners of the gym, exercises are posted on the wall. Do each exercise five times and then move to the next corner. And remember: This is not a race!"

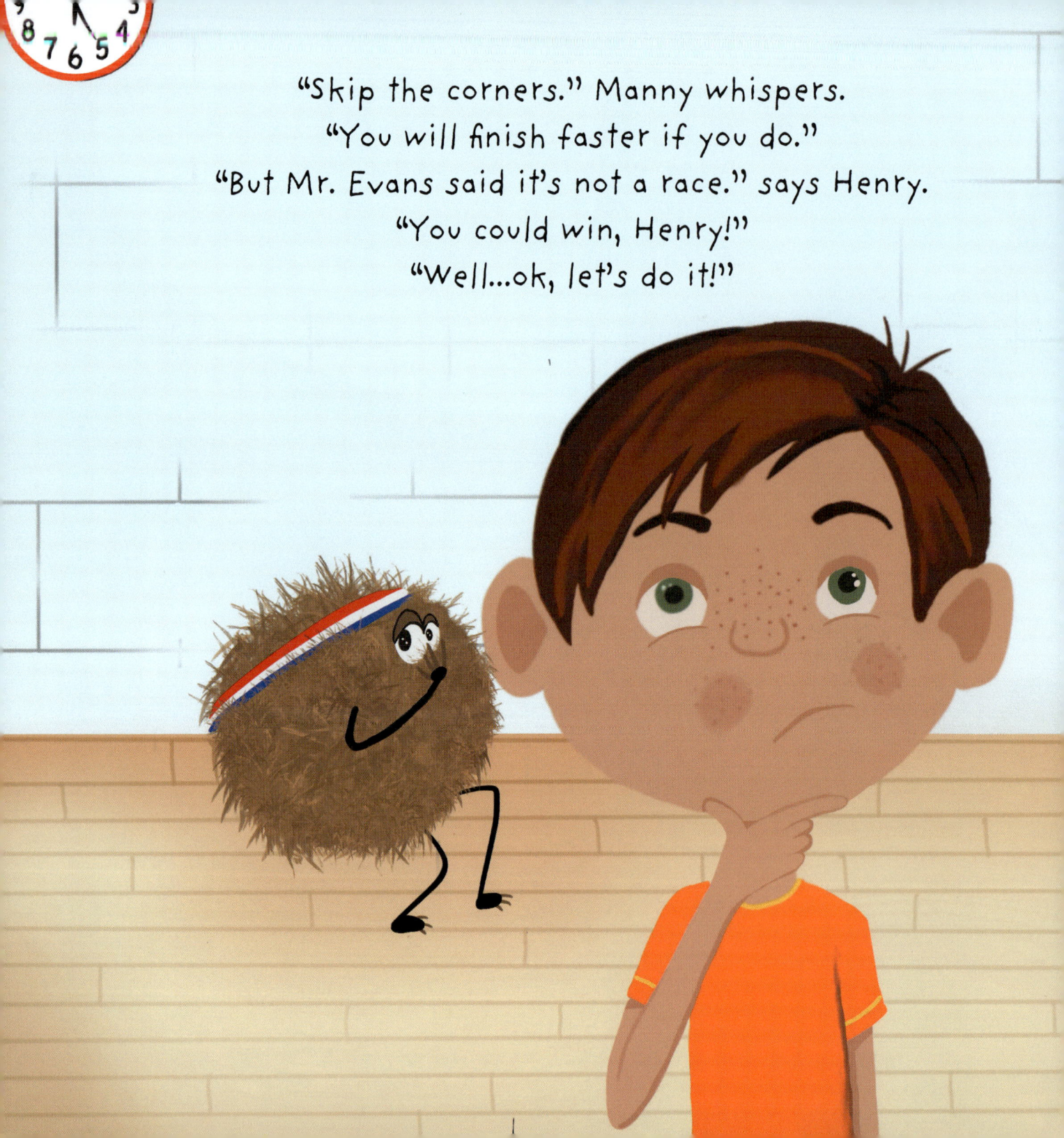

"Skip the corners." Manny whispers.
"You will finish faster if you do."
"But Mr. Evans said it's not a race." says Henry.
"You could win, Henry!"
"Well...ok, let's do it!"

Henry skips the first corner, zooms past the second and zips by the third. But as he approaches the final corner...

CRA

SH!!!

"Henry, you ignored my directions," says Mr. Evans." "It's not my fault! It was Manny."

"I don't want to hear any more about Manny. That's strike TWO!"

"Next, we're going to play 'Collect Five.' You need to collect high fives from five different people," explains Mr. Evans. "Then you give me a high five and start again."

Easy, thinks Henry.
He breaks into a run, but...

...All of his classmates sprint past him.

"High five them even if they're not looking!" says Manny.
Henry frowns, "I'm not sure..."
His feet carry him forward.
He zigs to the left.
He zags to the right...

SMACK!

Mr. Evans blows the whistle.
"Ouch! Henry pushed me!"

WALL SITS

"Henry, why did you push Eli?" asks Mr. Evans.
"It isn't my fault! Manny told me to..."
"Strike three. Go chill in the safe zone."

Henry shifts under the weight of his monster. "This doesn't feel right. I shouldn't be listening to you.

"Hahahahaha!!!"
"What are you laughing at?" asks Henry.
"I don't want you around anymore!"

"Oh, I'm not going anywhere," assures Manny.
"You did those things in class, not me."
"But...but...but you told me to."

"You don't get it, do you?" asks Manny. "That's my job. You mess up, I get bigger. Look at me! I'm HUGE!"

"Now I'm SURE this doesn't feel right," says Henry.

Laughter ripples through the room as Henry's classmates collect their high fives.
"I wish I could be out there too," mumbles Henry.

"Eli, wait!" yells Henry.
Eli stares straight ahead, and clenches his fists.
"Eli, STOP!"
Eli screeches to a halt.

"Your shoelace is untied," says Henry.
"Oh! Um, thanks," says Eli, stooping to tie his laces.
"And Eli...I'm sorry I crashed into you. I was mad that everyone ignored me," says Henry.
"I'm sorry too, friends?"
Henry grinned, "Friends."

"Whew. That felt great!"
says Henry.

POP!

"Speak for yourself. Don't do it again!" shouts Manny.
"Ok Henry, get back out there!" says Mr. Evans.

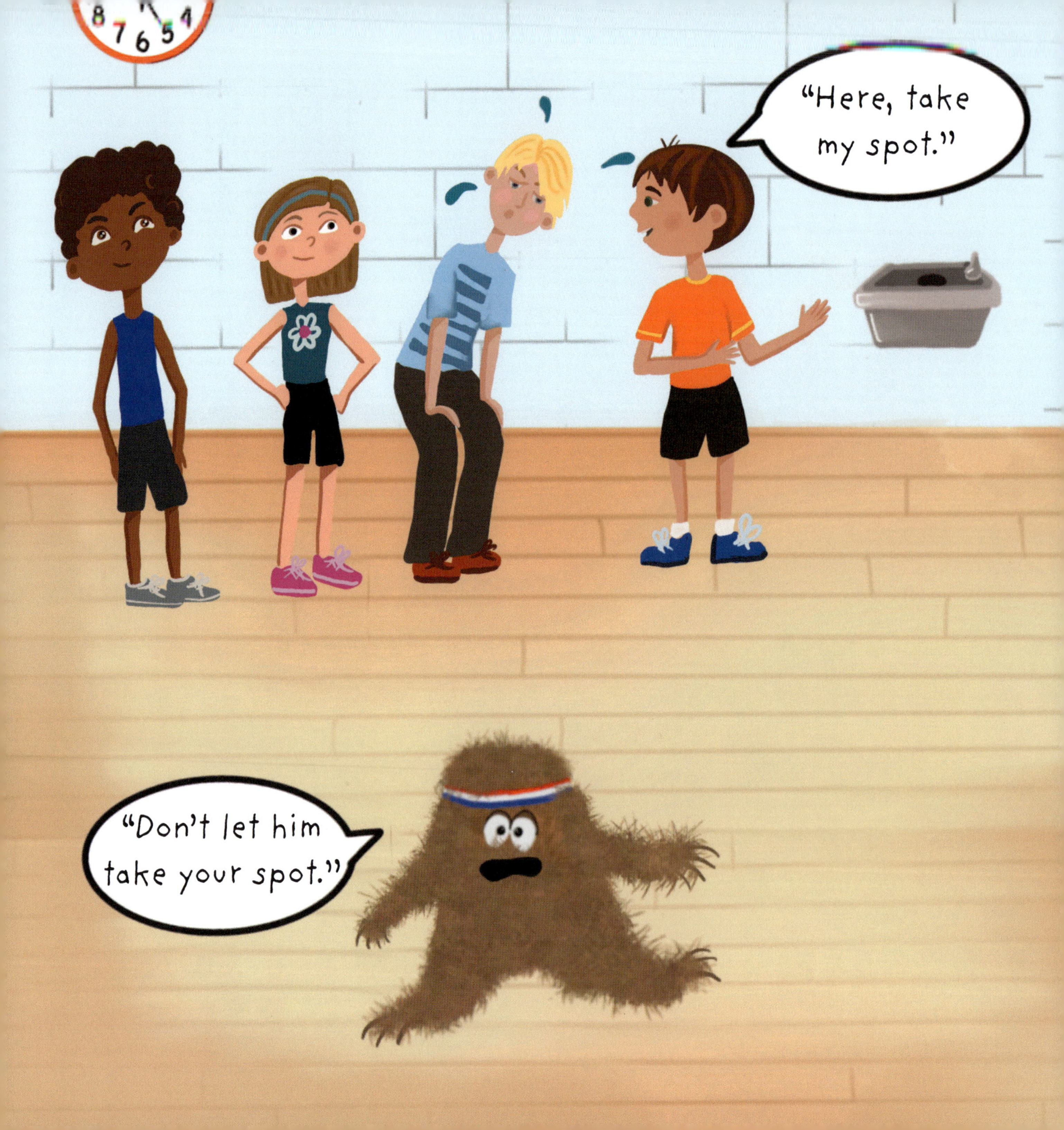
"Here, take my spot."
"Don't let him take your spot."

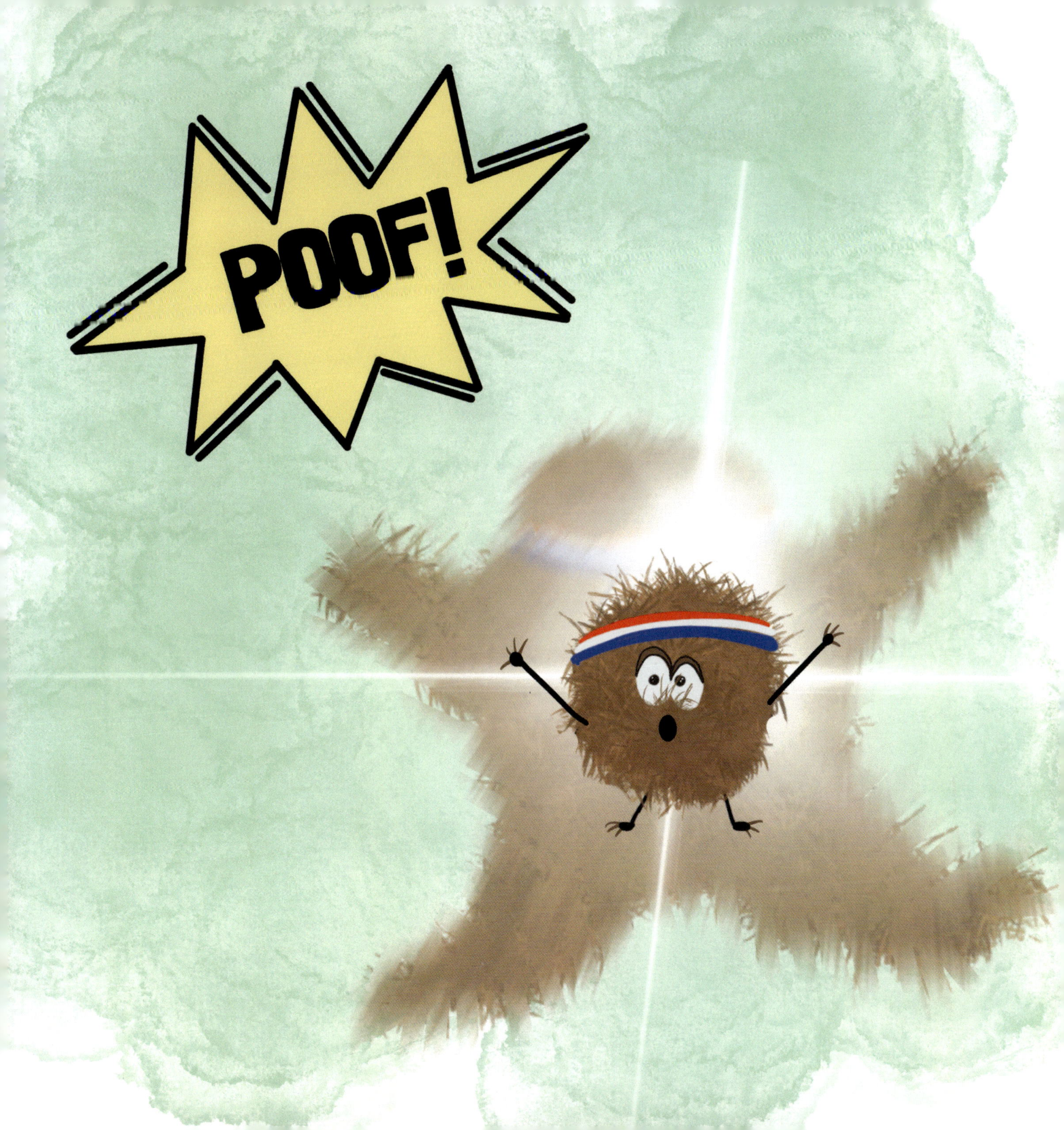
POOF!

JUMPING JACKS

"You ok?"

"Forget him! We have games to play!"

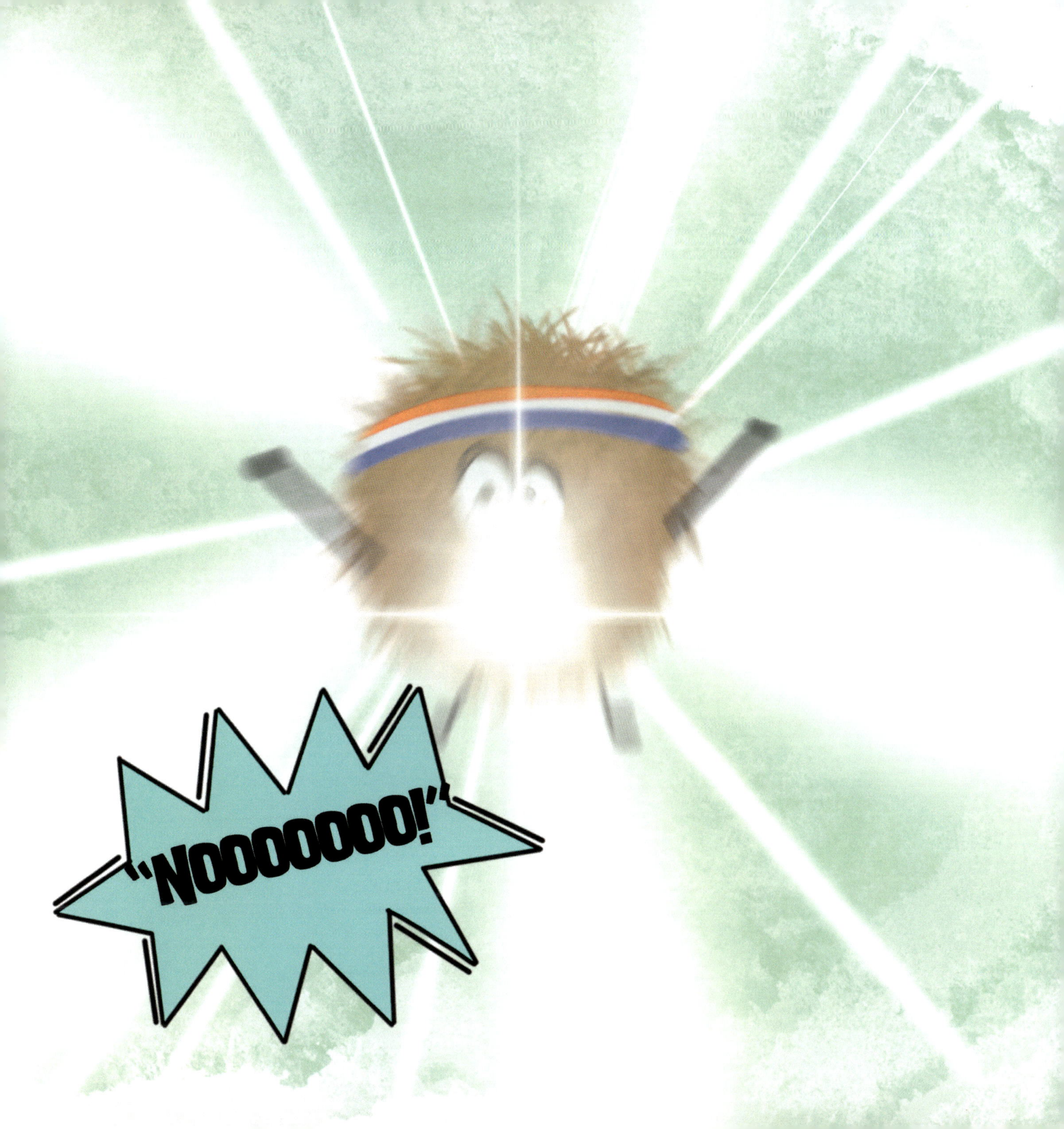
"NOOOOOOO!"

"See you all next week!"
"Guess what Mr. Evans? Manny is gone!" says Henry.
"I'm sorry I blamed him."
The teacher grinned and held up a hand.
"Now that deserves a high five!"

Back in the classroom, Henry flops down in his seat.
His desk begins to shake...

"Oh no, not the math minions!"

About the Author

Ben Lancour has had a passion for physical education since he began kindergarten at age five, which inspired him to subsequently earn a Bachelor's Degree in Physical Education from the University of Wisconsin-Oshkosh.

He is a husband and father of two children who love books. He was inspired to start writing because he saw a lack of picture books that teach social skills in the gym setting. He also hopes that this book encourages educators and parents to have discussions with their children about taking responsibility, no matter where it needs to take place.

About the Illustrator

Emily Bennett is a high school science teacher and varsity volleyball coach. She lives in Appleton where she enjoys restoring her 100-year old home and creating art.

She has always had a passion for science and art and believes that kids should be free to pursue multiple passions. Emily loves utilizing her science background in her art and taking the time to truly understand the details of her subject matter.

Your kids will love the digital read aloud. Check it out and get FREE coloring pages at

www.benlancourbooks.com

Email me idea freebies you'd like to see at:
LANCOB42@GMAIL.COM

Printed in Great Britain
by Amazon